D0733723

*Overdrive*
published in 2009 by
Hardie Grant Egmont
Ground Floor, Building 1, 658 Church Street
Richmond, Victoria 3121, Australia
www.hardiegrantegmont.com.au

A CiP record for this title is available from the National Library of Australia

Text copyright © 2009 H.I. Larry
Illustration and design copyright © 2009 Hardie Grant Egmont

Cover design & illustrations by Dan McDonald
Typeset by Ektavo

Printed in Australia by Griffin Press, an Accredited ISO AS/NZS
14001:2004 Environmental Management System printer.

3 5 7 9 10 8 6 4

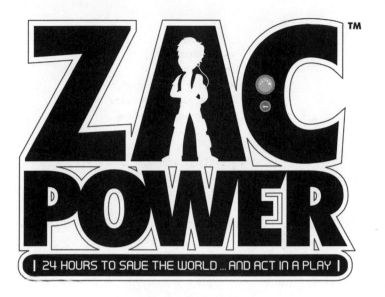

**ZAC POWER**™

| 24 HOURS TO SAVE THE WORLD ... AND ACT IN A PLAY |

# *OVERDRIVE*

## BY *H. I. LARRY*

### *ILLUSTRATIONS BY* **DAN McDONALD**

**hardie grant** EGMONT

# CHAPTER ...ONE

*This isn't a school musical*, Zac Power fumed to himself. *This is a crime against my ears!*

It was the final dress rehearsal for Zac's school musical and he was listening to the school choir practise. Opening night was only 24 hours away.

'The choir needs 24 years to practise, not 24 hours,' Zac muttered to himself.

He was standing backstage, waiting for his turn to go on. 'They're so terrible they'd shatter glass – in Siberia!'

The theme of the musical was protecting the environment. It was a good cause, but Zac was dreading the show.

Zac had a leading role – and that meant he had to sing a solo! The song was called 'I'm an Okey-Dokey Oak Tree'.

It was 7.06 p.m. – almost time for Zac's solo.

Zac was dressed in his costume, a huge

head-to-toe oak tree. It was decorated with acorns and a fake possum. Zac's face poked through the front of the tree trunk. His Rapido X-Fire sneakers stuck out underneath. But the absolute worst part was that the suit pinned Zac's arms to his side. He couldn't even scratch his nose.

*This is so embarrassing!* Zac thought. *I am a top international super spy, after all.*

Zac was twelve, and he had an awesome job with the Government Investigation Bureau (or GIB for short). His code name was Agent Rock Star. Zac's mum and dad were spies too. Even his big brother Leon worked for GIB. Leon worked in the Tech Support and Gadget Design Division.

AGENT / ZAC POWER
SPY NAME / AGENT ROCK STAR
AGE / 12

SCAN HERE >>>

Leon was doing sound and lighting for the school musical. But right then, he was backstage next to Zac, flipping through a newspaper.

'Some miners have struck a massive gold deposit in a town called Monteforte,' Leon said, holding up the paper. 'It says here that all the banks are absolutely stuffed with gold.'

'Isn't Monteforte where the Formula

One Grand Prix is held?' Zac asked.

Leon nodded and went back to reading.

On stage, the choir got louder and louder. It could only mean one thing – the choir's song was almost over.

'At last,' Zac whispered to Leon as he got ready to walk on stage. 'My eardrums were about to explode!'

Just then, something thumped the back of Zac's tree costume.

Zac couldn't see what it was, but he wasn't bothered. *Guess the teachers are checking that the pulley's working.*

The school hall had a pulley hanging down from the ceiling. It clipped onto a special loop on Zac's costume. When Zac finished his solo, he was going to be raised up off the stage. It was supposed to look like the oak tree was being uprooted.

'Fa-la-la-LA-la-la-la!' Zac sung to himself under his breath.

*Got to warm up my voice,* he thought. *If I'm singing a solo, I want to sound decent.*

# WHOOSH!

'HEY!' Zac yelled, as he was suddenly lifted off the ground. 'What's going on?'

Zac sped towards the ceiling. 'Leon!' he called. 'The lift shouldn't happen until *after* my solo!'

But Zac was already too high in the air. Leon couldn't help him.

A second later, a freezing wind slapped

Zac in the face. Zac twisted his neck around and looked up. It was tough to see in the tree suit. But Zac could tell that he was outside! He had been pulled through a skylight. And he wasn't hanging from the pulley in the school hall. He was dangling from a massive yellow crane!

The crane groaned into gear, swinging Zac over towards the school gates. And it was moving fast!

Zac swung back and forth as the crane picked up speed. He tried desperately to wriggle free of the oak tree costume. But that only swung him around more.

Zac started to feel sick from all the jolting around. But even though he felt queasy, his spy brain was whirring.

*When GIB want me for a mission, they sometimes come and grab me unexpectedly,* thought Zac. *But still, I usually travel in style!*

Zac thought of all the stealth jets, super bikes and cool high-speed vehicles he'd travelled in.

*I've never, ever travelled in a crane,* Zac thought grimly. *A crane doesn't seem like GIB's style.*

That left Zac with a big question.

*If GIB didn't bust me through the school hall's roof, who did?*

# CHAPTER ...TWO

The crane suddenly stopped moving. It was lowering Zac down.

Dangling from the crane, Zac twisted around in his tree costume to get a better look.

A logging truck was parked just outside the school gates. It was piled with chopped-down trees.

*Looks like I'm the next tree to be loaded*, thought Zac. Then he heard a soft click.

## WHOOSH!

The crane released Zac ten metres from the ground!

Zac let himself go floppy, like he'd learnt in spy school. A split second later, he landed on the truck, flat on his back. His stiff tree costume smacked down hard on the pile of logs.

## OOOOF!

Zac felt the logging truck rumble to life and take off. Zac had no idea where he was going. All he could see was the starry sky above him.

*I'd better call Leon for help*, thought Zac.

Zac needed to use his SpyPad to call Leon. SpyPads were the powerful mini-computers that all GIB spies carried. As well as having high-tech spy programs, SpyPads had a mobile phone function. Plus they had loads of cool games. *F1 Legends* was one of Zac's favourites.

Zac moved to grab his SpyPad from his pocket, where he always kept it. But he didn't get far. Thanks to his tree costume, his arms were pinned to his sides.

Zac groaned. For once in his spy career, he was helpless. It was the worst feeling in the world. There was nothing to do but lie there like a lump of wood.

The truck ride seemed to last forever.

At one point, the truck drove inside somewhere, and Zac thought it had finally stopped. All he could see was a black roof above his head. But even though the truck itself wasn't moving, it still seemed to rock from side to side.

*It's exactly like being at sea,* thought Zac. *The truck must be on a cargo ship!*

Then at last the side-to-side movement stopped. The truck drove down a ramp. Zac had a view of the night sky again.

Then an eerie sound filled the air.

*It sounds like a million angry mutant mosquitoes about to attack,* Zac thought.

The truck's cabin door slammed. Zac heard heavy footsteps crunching on gravel.

Every muscle in his body clenched.

*I'm about to come face-to-face with my kidnapper!* he thought, preparing himself.

The footsteps stopped. There was a chilling silence. Then...

'Right-oh, Agent Rock Star,' said a cheerful voice. 'We're here!'

*The truck driver knows my spy name!*

A second later, a sweaty face was staring down at Zac from above.

'I'm Agent Rusty Bassoon, from the GIB Marching Band,' said the man. 'Er, I mean, I'm your GIB driver. I've just been transferred.'

Zac looked at him suspiciously. *I didn't know GIB had a marching band!*

There was one quick way to check if Rusty was telling the truth.

'If you're an agent, then where's my mission?' said Zac.

Rusty bent down and plucked an acorn from the top branch of Zac's tree costume. 'You mean this?' he asked.

Immediately, Zac spotted something unusual about the acorn. There was a tiny speaker on one side of it.

'Ah, it's a DNA-Protected Audio Mission Device,' Zac explained to Rusty. 'I lick it and it checks my DNA. If my DNA matches, it plays my next mission.'

Rusty held the acorn close so Zac could lick it.

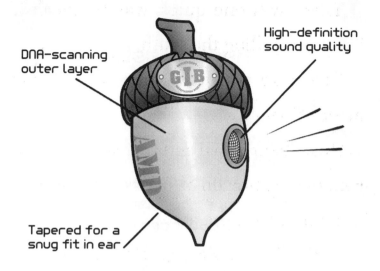

High-definition
sound quality

DNA-scanning
outer layer

Tapered for a
snug fit in ear

**G.I.B. AUDIO MISSION DEVICE**
**DNA-protected Message Recorder**

'Now put it in my ear,' said Zac. He tried not to wince as the spit-covered acorn squelched into his ear. Gross!

'Scanning DNA...' murmured a robotic voice in Zac's ear. 'Approved!'

Then the mission recording played.

# GIB Audio Mission

For Agent Rock Star's ears only

MISSION INITIATED: 11.00 a.m. Thursday

Tomorrow is the Formula One Grand Prix at Monteforte. GIB has heard that a new racing team will drive the fastest car in the world. Sources say the car goes 100km faster than any other vehicle. Yet this racing team is unheard of and doesn't even have any sponsors.

GIB suspects the racing team is up to something else in Monteforte.

Your mission:
Investigate the new racing team and their ultra-fast car.

Zac listened closely. Then he frowned. 'This message says my mission started at 11 a.m.,' he said to Rusty. 'Why did it take so long to get it to me?'

'Umm…well,' Rusty stammered. 'I… I got lost,' he finished lamely.

'You got lost?!' Zac was annoyed. 'Well, can you hurry up and help me out of this costume?'

'Sorry, Agent Rock Star,' said Rusty. 'You'll have to stay in the costume a little longer. It's a useful disguise.'

*I thought singing a solo was embarrassing,* Zac moaned to himself. *This is a billion times worse!*

He was annoyed that Rusty had cost

him so much time. 'If we were running late, why didn't we fly instead of –'

'Um, Agent Rock Star?' interrupted Rusty.

'What?' Zac snapped.

'That acorn in your ear. It's...well, it's smoking.'

*Smoking? Oh no!* Zac had forgotten one important detail.

DNA-Protected AMDs were always programmed to self-destruct. The listening device was about to explode in Zac's ear!

# CHAPTER... ...THREE

Zac was still flat on his back and trapped in the tree costume. He took a deep breath to calm the panic rising in him.

'Listen carefully,' Zac told Rusty. 'You'll have to grab the acorn and chuck it as far as you can.'

Fumbling a little, Rusty plucked the AMD from Zac's ear. He threw it well away from them.

The minute it touched the ground...

## KER-BOOM!

The acorn exploded in a cloud of dust. Pieces of the device shot in all directions.

'Great throw, Rusty,' said Zac, relieved.

'Years of practice twirling batons in the GIB Marching Band,' smiled Rusty modestly.

*Who'd have thought something as uncool as a marching band would be so useful?* Zac thought.

'Right,' said Zac. 'I've got my mission. Now I'd better get on with it! What's the time?'

Rusty consulted his watch.

'It's 1.53 a.m. Time to get you closer to the race-track,' he said.

*We're already near the track*, realised Zac. *That noise I heard before wasn't angry mosquitoes. It was Formula One race-cars.*

'Ready, Agent Rock Star?' asked Rusty.

'Ready,' said Zac.

With that, Rusty rolled Zac and his tree costume down the side of the log truck. At the bottom, Rusty picked up Zac and hoisted him onto his shoulders.

Zac had a good view of the Monteforte Race-track from Rusty's shoulders. Massive floodlights lit the track like it was the middle of the day.

The Monteforte Grand Prix was the next day, so the teams were frantic with final preparations. Mechanics swarmed like ants around their cars. Drivers strutted along in helmets and fireproof jumpsuits. There was even a team of gardeners clipping the grass alongside the track.

But most impressive of all were the F1 cars themselves. The cars were brightly painted, low to the ground and looked seriously fast. Each had a number and the racing team's name on the side.

From up on Rusty's shoulders, Zac noticed one car in particular. It was a brilliant blood red. The car's engine seemed to snarl and roar even louder than the others.

*I'm driving that car if it's the last thing I do on this mission,* vowed Zac to himself.

There was a name on the car's rear spoiler.

## TEAM D'ARGENT

Luckily for Zac, the crowds at the race-track were too excited to pay any attention to him. Rusty put Zac's tree down at the edge of the race-track and then slipped away before anyone realised he'd planted a top GIB spy in their midst.

*My first task is to work out which of these cars is ultra-fast,* thought Zac. He scanned the track closely for evidence.

The cars were doing practice laps, getting to know the course before tomorrow's race. Cars shot past Zac in a blur of colour.

*Each one of these cars seems as fast as the others,* thought Zac, frustrated. *How am I ever going to tell…*

## ZOOOOM!

Suddenly the blood-red car flashed by. Its engine roared like a rampaging dinosaur.

The car was so fast it made the others look like grannies with walking sticks.

*It's Team D'Argent,* Zac told himself. *And that must be the world's fastest car.*

Then Zac spotted something else. Dark liquid had pooled on the track, just ahead of a sharp turn. It was the exact turn where Zac's tree was positioned…

*An oil slick*, thought Zac. *If the D'Argent car drives over it, it'll lose control. It might crash into me!*

The blood-red car hurtled into the sharp turn. The noise of the engine hammered at Zac's brain.

Zac knew that his life was in danger. The instinct to run was powerful.

*But I can't run in this suit,* Zac thought with calm spy logic. *And giving up my hiding place will compromise the mission.*

Zac decided to stay put. Like it or not, he was about to go head-to-head with the world's fastest car.

# CHAPTER ... ... FOUR

Team D'Argent's car zoomed towards the oil slick. In a split second, it would spin out of control.

The image of a fireball of petrol and smoke flashed into Zac's mind. But he forced himself to stay cool as —

## SCREEEEECH!

Tyres squealed and the engine roared

as the driver shifted the gears down and slammed on the brakes. The blood-red car stopped millimetres away from the oil slick!

*How can a car going that fast stop so suddenly?* Zac gasped.

People in matching red uniforms came running from all directions.

'Ze brakes are magnifique!' said a voice with a foreign accent.

'It will be veeery useful on Wednesday,' said another.

*Wednesday? The Grand Prix is tomorrow,* thought Zac at once. *And tomorrow's Friday.*

It looked like GIB was right. Team D'Argent were up to something other than trying to win the Monteforte Grand Prix!

'Who planted zat stupid tree on zis sharp turn?' asked a member of Team D'Argent, looking over at Zac in his tree costume. 'It is too dangerous.'

The other voices muttered in agreement. Then…

'I 'ave a chainsaw,' called a voice. 'I'll get rid of it.'

## RRR-RRRRRRRRR-RRR!

The sound chilled Zac to the core. The chainsaw was getting closer by the second! *I'll have to run for it now,* Zac thought grimly.

There wasn't much wiggle room inside

the tree costume. Zac had never taken it off on his own before. He might have enough room to haul the suit over his head.

Pressing his hands against the trunk, Zac heaved upwards. The costume moved about a millimetre.

**RRR-RRRRRRRRR-RRR!**

The chainsaw buzzed in Zac's ear. His stomach lurched.

Scraping together every shred of his strength, Zac pushed again.

This time, he hauled the suit right over his head. It fell to the ground with a thud. Zac was surrounded by the members of Team D'Argent.

Not one of them moved. They were so

surprised to see Zac appear from inside a tree, they were paralysed!

'Timber!' Zac yelled, bolting away as fast as he could. Any second, the men would come to their senses.

Zac scanned for a hiding place as he ran. To his right was a row of pit garages. Cars stopped there for refuelling and tyre changes during Formula One races.

Zac glanced over his shoulder. Angry figures wearing red jumpsuits were coming after him.

He swerved towards the nearest pit garage. The walls were painted the same blood red.

Outside the garage was a fuel pump and

car lift for changing tyres. There was also an indoor garage. Luckily for Zac, the door was open. Zac ducked inside. And there, right in front of him, was a second ultra-fast race-car.

*Team D'Argent have two identical ultra-fast cars? Of course,* he realised. *All racing teams have back-up cars.*

Zac was drawn to the car like it was magnetic. It was incredible. He was stroking the shiny red paint when he heard something. Footsteps!

But Zac couldn't run out the way he'd come in. He would run directly into the men from Team D'Argent!

Then Zac spotted a door labelled Change

Room. He burst through the door.

*Yes!* The change room was full of lockers to hide in. A clock on the wall read:

But there was a problem. Someone else was already there!

The man was wearing a red jumpsuit. He held a gleaming red helmet.

*He must drive the second car,* thought Zac.

'What are you doing in 'ere, leetle boy?' the driver demanded.

*Little boy!* Zac clenched his fist. 'I'm… er…' he muttered.

Then a plan popped into Zac's mind.

He crouched down. 'Hang on,' he said. 'My shoelace's undone.'

The driver looked away, rolling his eyes. Zac seized his chance. He ripped off his left shoe and sock. Stitched into Zac's sock was a tiny tube of grey gas. Zac snapped the lid off the glass.

Zac held his breath. It was the only way to avoid breathing in the stench of sweaty football socks that was flooding the room. This powerfully disgusting gadget was Leon's latest invention. He called them Knock-Out Socks.

Zac pinched his nose shut for safety. and waved the Knock-Out Sock in the driver's face.

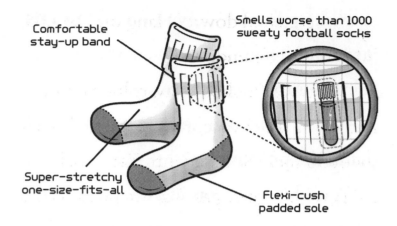

Comfortable stay-up band

Smells worse than 1000 sweaty football socks

Super-stretchy one-size-fits-all

Flexi-cush padded sole

G.I.B. KNOCK-OUT SOCKS
Coma-inducing Footwear

The driver screwed up his face. He swayed for a moment. Then he fainted, dropping to the ground.

Zac shut the stinking sock in a locker. He unzipped the driver's jumpsuit. The driver could wake up at any moment, so Zac didn't have long. He pulled off the man's jumpsuit and put it on. He stuffed everything from his own pockets into the jumpsuit. Then Zac shoved the driver's helmet onto his own head.

Just in time! He heard an angry voice out in the pit garage.

With his best confident swagger, Zac strolled out of the change room.

'Bonjour, Jacques,' a man said to Zac. He was dressed in the same red jumpsuit and was holding a helmet.

'Avez-vous vu un petit enfant?' the driver said.

*Uh-oh*, Zac thought. *He's speaking French. And I can't speak French!*

# CHAPTER ... FIVE

Zac's skin prickled. *If only I'd paid attention in GIB's Basic French for Spies*, he thought.

'Jacques, avez-vous vu un petit enfant?' repeated the driver coldly.

*Use spy logic to guess what he's asking*, Zac urged himself. *Then fudge an answer!*

The driver had just seen a boy run out of a tree. So…

*He's probably asking if I've seen a kid anywhere,* figured Zac. *At least, I hope he is!*

Zac shrugged dramatically. 'Non!' he said in his best French accent.

The driver continued speaking in rapid French, a dangerous tone in his voice.

Zac didn't understand a word.

If this French conversation went on any longer, the driver would guess that Zac was an impostor. Zac needed a plan – now!

Zac plunged his hands into the jumpsuit pockets. But there was nothing much in there. He hadn't got any new gadgets before this mission like he normally did.

Then his hand closed around a half-eaten lolly.

Suddenly, Zac remembered when he'd first sucked that lolly. At home, in Leon's underground lab.

*Leon said the lolly was a prototype instant translator!* Zac remembered, excited.

The lolly was covered in pocket fluff. But Zac flipped up his helmet visor and stuffed it into his mouth anyway.

'I haven't seen a kid,' said Zac straight

away. The Universal Gobstopper worked! Zac had just spoken in perfect French.

'I've been working on the car in here,' Zac continued in French.

The driver nodded. Zac felt so confident, he started to chat.

'I enjoy tap-dancing and eating salami sandwiches!' Zac said.

The driver raised his eyebrows in surprise.

*Uh-oh. Leon said the Universal Gobstopper was a prototype, so it might not work properly,* Zac thought. *That wasn't what I meant to say! Better change the subject.*

'It's after 3 a.m. I need to do some practice laps,' said Zac carefully in French.

Luckily the French came out right this time.

The driver nodded. In silence, he walked over to the car and motioned for Zac to climb in.

Zac had done some cool things on spy missions. But driving the world's fastest car was going to be the best!

Sliding into the low seat, Zac secured the harness around him. He punched the ignition button. A roar echoed around the garage. Zac put the car into gear and tapped the accelerator. The car shot forward. Zac charged out of the garage and onto the track.

Other drivers doing practice laps flew

past Zac. The whine was deafening.

## NEEEEEOOOOW!

Zac slammed the accelerator and moved up the gears. The speedo flew higher.

**200 kilometres.**
**300.**
**400.**
**450!**

None of the other cars was even close to being as fast as Zac. He lost all sense of his body. Of how fast he was driving. It was just him and the world's fastest car, powering forward. He was unstoppable!

Whooping, Zac thundered towards the sharp bend.

Playing *F1 Legends* had taught him about

braking into a corner. But Zac wasn't letting anything slow him down.

He flew into the bend. He was going fast...too fast!

All of a sudden, the back of the car was sliding. The tyres squealed.

## SCREEEEECH!

Through Zac's helmet visor, the world circled around and around.

*This is just like totalling a car in the F1 Legends game,* Zac thought numbly. *Only this time it's for real...*

# CHAPTER... ...SIX

Zac gripped the steering wheel, his knuckles white. The car spun sickeningly, like a roller-coaster ride gone terribly wrong.

*Must...not...crash...will...compromise... mission*, Zac thought dully.

Zac's eyes swam. The instruments on the dashboard were a blur. But one stood out. It was marked with a red arrow, pointing up. Zac reached out and stabbed the button.

Deep inside the car, the gears crunched. Jets of smoke shot out from either side of Zac's seat. The seat rumbled. Then...

Like a human champagne cork, Zac soared out of the car and into the air. He'd activated the ejector seat!

He glanced down as he flew through the air. Below, he saw the race-car crash into a pile of tyres beside the track. Its nose crumpled like paper. Axles snapped and the wheels hung at crazy angles. The car was a write-off!

Still strapped into the ejector seat,

Zac whistled upwards into the air. He looked for the parachute release button. But he couldn't find one anywhere. There was nothing but a strange lever on the side of the seat...

Zac yanked the lever. There was a whirring sound behind him. He looked around to see what was going on. A folding carbon-fibre propeller popped out from the top of the seat! The propeller began to spin.

*An ejector seat that converts into a mini-chopper?* Zac thought, puzzled.

Zac knew that all race-cars had an ejector seat to help drivers land safely on the ground in an accident. But why would

Team D'Argent need one that let drivers fly off into the air?

Zac's mind began to race. *Maybe Team D'Argent wants their drivers to escape from something other than a car crash...*

Whatever the point of it was, at least the mini-chopper was very cool, and easy to control. *Put all my weight to the left and I turn left*, Zac noticed. *Basic.*

High above the race-track, Zac had a perfect view of Monteforte in the early hours of the morning. Mansions with flood-lit swimming pools lined every street. Under the streetlights, Zac saw a bank on nearly every corner.

Suddenly Zac remembered the article

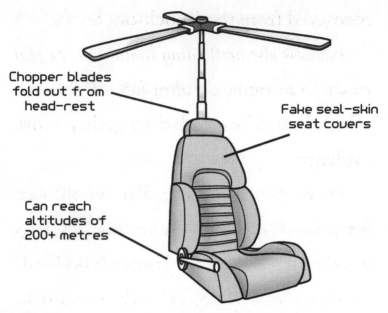

Chopper blades
fold out from
head-rest

Fake seal-skin
seat covers

Can reach
altitudes of
200+ metres

TEAM D'ARGENT MINI-CHOPPER EJECTOR SEAT

that Leon had read in the newspaper. *Those
banks will all be full of gold*, he thought.

Zac plotted his next move. *Going back
to the track is too risky*, he thought. By now,
Team D'Argent's second driver would have

recovered from the Knock-out Socks.

*But how else am I going to uncover the real reason for inventing the ultra-fast car?* Zac had a hunch, but he needed to gather more evidence.

From the chopper, Zac could see for miles. Up ahead, he noticed a lit-up warehouse. And it was painted blood red.

*That's Team D'Argent's colour!* thought Zac. But that didn't make sense. If Team D'Argent were like every other racing team, they didn't come from Monteforte. Most teams just came for the big race, and then left again once it was over. *There's no reason the team needs a warehouse here*, Zac reasoned. His spy senses tingled.

Zac spotted a thick clump of bushes near the warehouse and flew over to hover above them. Then he leant his body weight forward. Immediately, the mini-chopper tilted downwards. Zac landed in the bushes and unstrapped himself from the seat.

*Better check to see if anyone's hanging around*, Zac figured.

He reached in his pocket and pulled out a small plastic case. Inside was his Portascope. This gadget looked exactly like a contact lens, but the lens was telescopic.

Taking off his helmet, Zac slipped the Portascope onto his eye and turned to look at the warehouse. He was 50 metres away, but he could see through the window perfectly! It was like looking through a telescope.

Zac's heart sank. The warehouse was crawling with people in blood-red uniforms. There was no way Zac could get in with so many people around.

He checked his watch.

Creeping a little closer to the fence, Zac could just hear snatches of conversation between the people at the warehouse. Most of it was in French, but a few of the workers spoke English.

Zac kept an ear out for anything interesting, and to make use of the time, he plugged the word 'D'Argent' into his SpyPad's translation function.

*Weird name for a racing team*, thought Zac. *Why would they call themselves that?*

Then a voice cut into his thoughts.

'We have to hurry – we only have a couple of hours before they need everyone at the track,' one of the workers said.

*Yes!* That was what Zac wanted to hear.

He was sure the warehouse held the key to Team D'Argent's plans.

Slowly, the minutes crawled by.

4.47 a.m.... 5.51 a.m....

But at last the workers seemed to be leaving. When the last of them had disappeared from sight, Zac left the bushes cautiously. Sticking to the shadows, Zac sneaked towards the warehouse's front entrance. The place was surrounded by a three-metre high, barbed-wire fence.

*Team D'Argent really doesn't want anyone here*, thought Zac, spy senses on high alert.

Then something brushed Zac's leg. He heard a panting sound by his ankles.

Looking down, Zac saw a sausage dog. He reached down for a pat. He couldn't resist. The dog was pretty cute.

## YEEEE-OW!

The sausage dog bit Zac's hand! But instead of normal teeth, the dog's mouth was filled with steel pins!

*A Destruct-E-Dog!* Zac realised straight away. He remembered them from when Leon had made him read GIB's *Guide to Enemy Pets*. They were the toughest robotic guard dog ever invented.

The sound of pattering footsteps filled the air. *Uh-oh,* thought Zac. Looking around, he saw a whole family of Destruct-E-Dogs closing in.

# CHAPTER SEVEN

With their squat legs and perky ears, the Destruct-E-Dogs looked very cute.

*Until they flash their steel teeth at you,* Zac thought. He pressed hard on his hand to stop the bleeding.

Zac had to get past the Destruct-E-Dogs. He thought of all the things he knew about dogs.

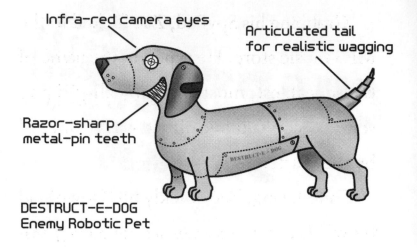

Infra-red camera eyes

Articulated tail
for realistic wagging

Razor-sharp
metal-pin teeth

DESTRUCT-E-DOG
Enemy Robotic Pet

Once, Zac and Leon had been watching music videos on TV. An all-girl band in glittery pink costumes came on. Zac's dog, Agent Woofy, ran out of the room with his tail between his legs. 'Dogs hate high frequencies,' Leon had said.

*Leon's nerdy facts do come in handy sometimes*, Zac admitted.

Grabbing his SpyPad, Zac flicked to the MP3 music store. He typed in the name of the squeakiest, most annoying all-girl pop song he could think off. It was 'Princess' by the Glitter Girlz.

Shuddering, Zac quickly hit 'Download Now'. *Lucky no-one can see me buying this terrible song!* he thought.

In seconds, the download was complete. Zac turned the volume right up and pressed play. A pair of shrill female voices filled the air.

*I've got a castle and it's painted pink,*

The Destruct-E-Dogs began a low growl.

*It's prettier and sparklier than you might think,*

It was too much for the Destruct-E-Dogs. Their robotic heads began to spin around. Sparks flew out of their ears. One by one, the dogs exploded in a giant cloud of fake fur.

*So that's the reason such horrible music exists*, thought Zac, grinning.

Leaving the bits of robotic dogs behind, Zac scaled the barbed wire fence and dropped lightly down on the other side. He sneaked towards the warehouse.

*They didn't think anyone would get past the dogs and the fence*, Zac thought, creeping inside the warehouse.

There didn't seem to be anyone around. Despite himself, Zac hummed the tune to 'Princess'.

But what he saw in the warehouse made him stop mid-tune.

Stretched out in front of him was an assembly-line of car parts. But the parts didn't belong to ordinary cars. There were race-car spoilers. Perfectly smooth racing tyres. Chopper-enabled ejector seats.

*Team D'Argent doesn't only have TWO*

*race-cars,* Zac thought. *They've got a factory full of them!*

It didn't make sense. Zac knew Team D'Argent couldn't possibly be racing all these cars.

*So what are they doing with them?* Zac wondered. He spotted an office nearby and pushed open the door. TV screens lined the walls. Each grainy image was labelled in white.

## LIVE FEED
## 7:04am
## FIRST NATIONAL BANK
## OF MONTEFORTE

'Security camera footage from bank vaults!' whispered Zac. Gold was piled high in every single vault.

He whipped around. Behind him on a table were some large sheets of paper. Blueprints for every major bank in Monteforte!

Next to the blueprints was a list of dates, times and addresses. The first date on the list was the next Wednesday.

Zac considered the evidence he'd gathered so far. Images of bank vaults. A car factory in Monteforte, one of the world's richest places. And a racing team with a name that meant 'Money'.

The answer was obvious.

Team D'Argent had created the fastest getaway cars in the world! And even if the robbery went wrong, the robbers could just fly off in the mini-choppers.

*Team D'Argent must be planning to rob every bank in Monteforte,* Zac thought. *Maybe that's what this list is for! But that means the first robbery is on Wednesday.*

It was an evil plan. Would Zac be able to stop it?

# CHAPTER EIGHT

Zac had no idea how to stop one robbery, let alone lots. He leant thoughtfully against a stack of boxes.

## INSTA-DRY EXTRA STRONG SILICONE SEALANT

Zac knew that silicone was a rubbery material used to seal things like car windows. *Maybe I could use it to seal other things,* Zac thought. *Like…every door and window in this warehouse!*

He ripped open a box. The silicone sealant came in tubes with a nozzle on top. Zac squeezed one and silicone oozed out.

Zac raced to a nearby window. He squirted silicone around the entire window frame. For a few nervous seconds, Zac waited. Then…

*Yes!* Zac tried to open the window, but it wouldn't budge. The silicone had set like cement. The window was sealed shut – for good! Zac ran to the next window along.

## SSSSSSQUT!

With a few quick squirts of silicone, he sealed the window. One by one, Zac closed up every window in the warehouse.

It was a long and exhausting job. The chemicals in the silicone stung Zac's eyes.

But by 8.48 a.m., Zac only had one door left to seal. It was the delivery entrance, a roller door at the back of the warehouse.

He started squirting silicone around the door-frame.

'Duh!' he laughed, suddenly stopping. 'I was about to seal myself inside the warehouse!'

Zac opened the door and stepped out. He slammed the door shut and sealed it.

*They might be able to break the windows,* Zac thought. *But there's no way any cars are leaving this warehouse.*

But there was one thing Zac still needed to do. He had to secure the other race-car that he'd seen at the track.

Just then Zac's SpyPad beeped. It was a mission update from Leon. Maybe he would have some more information.

But Zac's shoulder's sagged as he read.

*Where on earth is the most secure place at the*

MISSION UPDATE
MESSAGE
RECEIVED 9.07 A.M.

I hacked into
Team D'Argent's email.
They said that the
blueprints for the car
are being held at the
most secure place at
Monteforte Race-track.

I don't have any more
info – sorry! Good luck.

–Agent Tech Head

*track?* Zac wondered, racking his brains.

*Wait*, thought Zac. *All those cars – they're here to win the Monteforte Cup!*

Zac had heard that the Monteforte Cup was guarded day and night by security guards. The cup was never left alone.

*The cup has got to be the most secure thing at Monteforte!* Zac figured. *The plans must be near the cup, or even inside it.*

With such tight security, it would be almost impossible for Zac to get his hands on the cup. *Unless,* thought Zac, *I'm handed the cup on the winners' podium…*

And that would mean winning the Monteforte Grand Prix!

Zac dialled Leon's number at top speed. 'Leon?' he said urgently. 'Can you find me a car to race in the Grand Prix?'

'What? No! And you haven't practised!' said Leon.

'Yes, I have,' said Zac. But he didn't add that the last time he'd driven a Formula

One car, he'd crashed.

'It's the only way to complete the mission!' said Zac firmly.

'OK, Zac. A car will be waiting for you at the track,' Leon replied with a sigh. 'The race starts in 48 minutes.'

Zac gulped. This was going to be the drive of his life!

# CHAPTER NINE

Team D'Argent's warehouse was close to a busy main road. Zac hailed a taxi. Compared to a race-car, it was painfully slow, but he didn't have a choice. Taking the mini-chopper would draw too much attention.

Zac was excited, but he also felt more and more nervous as he neared the track.

Winning the Grand Prix wouldn't be easy, especially racing against the world's fastest car.

*Leon's right. How can I win when I haven't practised?*

True skill only came about by doing something over and over again.

*That's how I got so good at F1 Legends*, Zac thought.

Wait…*F1 Legends!* Zac was an expert at the racing game. In fact, he was one of the all-time top scorers in the online *F1 Legends Hall of Fame.*

*That's it!* thought Zac. *I'll take the skills I've learnt playing F1 Legends and apply them to the real-life race.*

Zac's stomach squelched with nerves and excitement as the taxi pulled to a stop. He'd arrived at Monteforte Race-track. And he was about to drive in an actual Grand Prix! He checked the time.

A man dressed in a cleaner's uniform sidled up to Zac.

'Greetings, incredible boy,' the cleaner said.

Zac rolled his eyes. Now was NOT the time to chat with a crazy person!

'Greetings, incredible boy,' the cleaner

repeated firmly.

Suddenly, Zac got it. The first letters of 'Greetings, incredible boy' were G, I and B! The cleaner was a GIB agent.

'Which one's my car?' whispered Zac.

The agent whisked Zac to a garage at the very end of the pits. A car was covered with a dust sheet.

The car underneath was low and sleek. And it was completely covered in gold glitter. It was so sparkly, Zac had to shade his eyes.

'Not the kind of car we'd normally give a secret agent,' the agent apologised.

'Short notice,' Zac said with a shrug. 'I understand.'

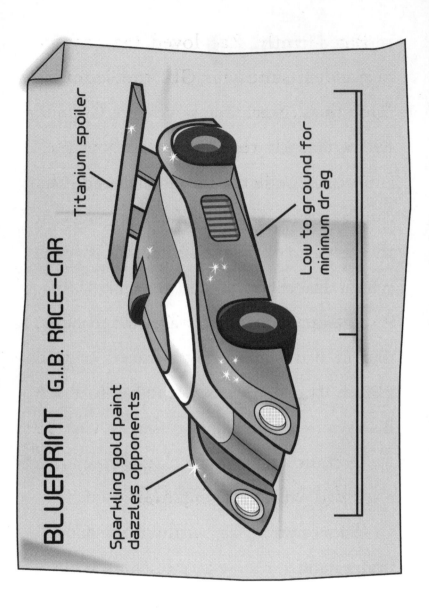

BLUEPRINT G.I.B. RACE-CAR

Titanium spoiler

Low to ground for minimum drag

Sparkling gold paint dazzles opponents

But secretly, Zac loved the glittery race-car. It suited his GIB code name — Agent Rock Star!

Zac quickly changed into a new suit, jammed on a helmet and got inside the car. It was so tiny that Zac's knees were up around his elbows. The dashboard was crammed with dials and blinking lights. It was all pretty cool. But Zac had to admit that Team D'Argent's car was cooler... and surely faster.

Suddenly, there was that sound of super-powered mosquitoes again.

## VROOOOOOOOOM!

It was the engines of the other Grand Prix cars! The race was about to start.

Zac started his engine too. He revved the engine up to 20,000 rpm. It was so loud he thought his ears might bleed.

Zac pressed his sneaker to the floor and raced onto the track. The other cars were lined up to start. Zac saw an empty slot at the start line reserved for him. He pulled into it with seconds to spare.

The lights above the start line counted down to the start of the race.

**RED...**
**AMBER...**
**GREEN!**

Zac slammed down on the accelerator.

**NEEEEEOOOOW!**

He took off so fast his vision went

blurry. The only thing he could see clearly was what was in front of his car. The rest of the world vanished as he focused on the track ahead.

'This is INSANE!' Zac yelled. Cars swerved and weaved in front of each other. Team D'Argent's car shot to the front of the track immediately. The blood-red car swerved dangerously around the other cars, almost causing a huge pile-up.

Zac accelerated through the pack. He hurtled around corners, remembering what he'd learnt playing *F1 Legends*.

*Keep wide. Hug the edge of the track,* he told himself. *Turn hard through the corner, come out wide. And hang on!*

*Yes!* Zac took a perfect racing line around the corner. And he found himself passing even more cars.

His confidence was growing with every corner he nailed. Zac kept passing cars like they were standing still.

Before long, he was overtaking cars he'd already passed once. Zac was a whole lap ahead of the other cars!

Well, all the cars except for one.

The blood-red beast belonging to Team D'Argent tore further and further in front. It showed no signs of slowing, despite being several laps ahead of Zac.

If anything, the D'Argent driver was driving even more dangerously than he had at the beginning of the race.

Zac wrestled with the steering wheel. His arms burned with exhaustion. He had his foot planted so hard on the accelerator that his leg ached with cramps.

Then Zac saw two cars narrowly avoid a collision as they spun out of the red car's way. The Team D'Argent driver was putting the other drivers at risk!

Zac realised he didn't just have to beat Team D'Argent to get the blueprints and prevent the robberies. Zac had to stop them before someone got hurt!

*But how I am going to catch the fastest car ever invented?* he wondered. Then an idea jumped into his mind.

He took his foot off the accelerator.

*This feels wrong,* he thought. *But I'm going for it anyway.*

Instantly, Zac's car slowed down. Soon he was like a grandpa on a Sunday drive. Never in Grand Prix history had a car driven so slowly around the track.

**NEEOOW! NEEOOW!**

Car after car whipped passed Zac.

*This is majorly embarrassing*, Zac cringed. But it didn't matter if the other cars passed Zac. They were a whole lap behind him anyway.

Zac's plan was to let the Team D'Argent car get so far ahead that it lapped him. It was working. The red car was coming up behind him, closer and closer.

Zac took one hand off the wheel. From underneath his drive suit, he pulled a leather cord he wore around his neck.

Dangling from the cord was a flat metal disc. It looked like jewellery. But it was actually a gadget called the Portable Sun.

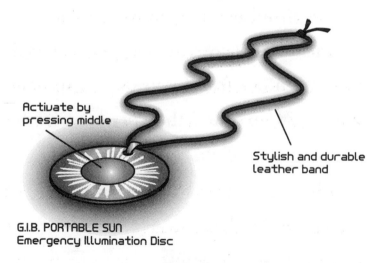

Activate by pressing middle

Stylish and durable leather band

G.I.B. PORTABLE SUN
Emergency Illumination Disc

Leon had given it to him a few weeks earlier. It was meant for spies trapped underground or in black-outs. But Zac had something different in mind.

He knew his plan was dangerous, but Team D'Argent was endangering too many people with their reckless driving. And Zac knew the red car had an ejector seat, so the driver would be able to escape.

Team D'Argent's car hurtled up behind Zac. With one hand still on the steering wheel, Zac pointed the Portable Sun out the window of his car and pressed the middle.

# CHAPTER ...TEN

Piercing white light shot out of the disc. Zac's aim was perfect! The powerful light beam flooded into Team D'Argent's car.

It was enough. For a second, Team D'Argent's driver was blinded. The blood-red car swerved off the road.

In his rear-view mirror, Zac saw the driver eject and zoom off into the air.

Seconds later, the car slammed into a barrier at the side of the track.

### *CRAAAASH!*

Glass shattered. Metal crumpled.

The car was a wreck. And with the warehouse sealed up, all of Team D'Argent's prototypes were gone.

In the middle of the chaos, a figure appeared by the side of the track. He was waving a chequered flag!

*That was the last lap*, Zac realised. He'd almost forgotten about the race. *I've done it! I've won the Monteforte Grand Prix!*

## NEEEEEOOOOW!

Zac gripped the steering wheel as he zoomed across the finish line.

Zac spun to a stop. Immediately, a cheering whooping crowd surrounded him.

Someone opened Zac's door and pulled him out of the car. Before Zac knew it, he was on the winner's podium, his helmet still on. Flashbulbs popped in his eyes. Someone shoved a microphone into his face. All around, voices were asking the same question.

'Who's the unknown driver that just won the Monteforte Grand Prix?'

Even though Zac knew he hadn't won fair and square, he was kind of enjoying the attention. *And Team D'Argent was driving way too dangerously,* he reasoned. *They needed to be stopped. They won't be robbing banks any time soon...*

'Let's see the winner holding the cup!' yelled a voice from the crowd.

A Grand Prix official appeared beside Zac. He handed Zac a gleaming silver cup.

Zac checked inside. The blueprints were there as expected, folded up into a tiny parcel. Hoping no-one would notice, he reached inside and grabbed the parcel.

Zac tucked the blueprints into his pocket. He'd deliver them to GIB later.

He held the cup high above his head. The cameras went crazy again.

Then Zac heard another voice from the crowd.

'Take off your helmet!' called another voice in the crowd. 'The world wants to see the latest F1 star!'

*Take off my helmet?* thought Zac. *Then everyone will see that I'm 12 years old!*

Plus, Zac knew that as a GIB spy, he had to keep his identity secret. The last thing he needed was his photo on the front page of every newspaper in the world!

'Take it off!' chanted the crowd.

Zac looked around for a way out. Then the Grand Prix official tapped him on the shoulder.

'Excuse me, sir,' whispered the official. 'A gift from Agent Tech Head.' He handed Zac a gigantic bottle of champagne.

Zac noticed something written in tiny print on top of the cork:

**SHAKE ME**

Zac shook the champagne bottle as hard as he could. Then he popped the cork.

## *BOOOOOOOM!*

Jets of frothy champagne sprayed twenty metres into the air. The crowd gasped as it was covered in a thick shower of champagne.

*Extra frothy champagne!* thought Zac. *Nice one, Leon.*

Zac leapt off the winner's podium. He plunged into the crowd, taking off his helmet as he ran and throwing it aside.

There were lots of kids dressed up, so he blended in.

*Being a normal kid would be good right*

*now*, thought Zac. *I could look around the track properly, see all the cars...*

Then Zac smiled to himself. *Why shouldn't I? My mission's complete, after all...*

But just then Zac's SpyPad beeped.

Zac groaned. It would take him ages to get to school from Monteforte Race-track.

*If I don't leave now, I might not make it home in time for my solo,* thought Zac.

His dad would be so disappointed. Zac couldn't do that to him. If he had to sing 'I'm an Okey-Dokey Oak Tree' in front of everyone he knew, that was the way it had to be.

Looking around to make sure no-one was watching, Zac jumped back in the GIB race-car. *At least I can drive this awesome car home,* he thought.

He cleared his throat. 'Fa-la-la-LA-la-la-la,' he sang, warming up to practise his solo on the way.

*I'm already an F1 legend*, he thought. *Got to make sure I'm a legendary oak tree too!*

## ... THE END ...

# MISSION CHECKLIST
## How many have you read?